# Amazing Space Facts

By Dinah L. Moché, Ph.D.
Illustrations by R. W. Alley

A GOLDEN BOOK • NEW YORK
Western Publishing Company, Inc., Racine, Wisconsin 53404

# STARS

Stars look like tiny sparkles in the night sky, but they are really huge shining balls of very hot gases. They look tiny because they are very, very far away. You would need to put trillions and trillions of basketballs together to make a ball as big as a star.

Light from the stars travels at the fastest speed possible: 670 million miles an hour. If you could travel at this speed—the speed of light—you would get to our moon in a second and a half. Even if you could travel at light speed, you would still need over four years to reach Alpha Centauri, one of our closest stars. Other stars would require an even longer trip.

There are billions and billions of stars in space.

When you look at the stars, you look into the past. Stars
are trillions of miles away from us, and it takes a very
long time for their light to reach Earth. By the time
starlight reaches your eyes, it has already traveled for
many years. So when you look at a star, you see how it
looked many years ago.

The constellation Orion

Stars in the same part of the sky may look as if they belong to groups when they're not really related at all. Long ago people named and made up stories about star patterns, which are called constellations. A famous one is Orion the Hunter.

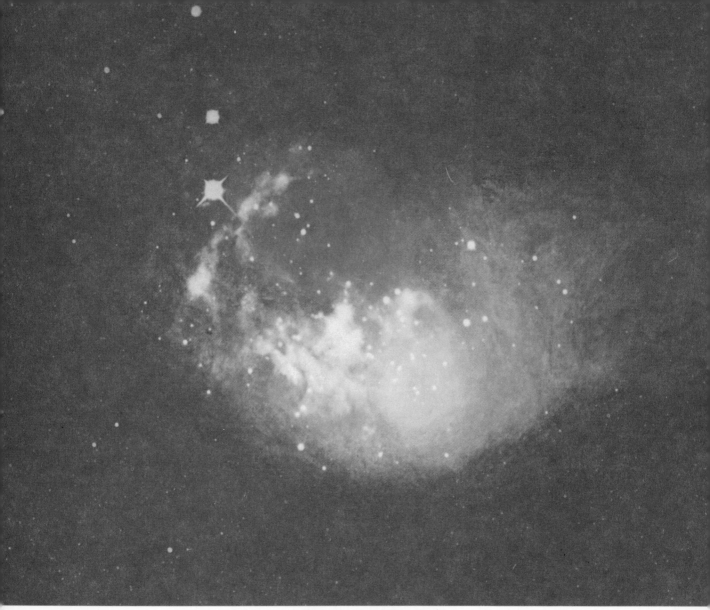

The Orion Nebula

Stars form in enormous clouds of gases and dust that are called nebulas. They shine for millions, even billions, of years, but no star shines forever. When their fuel is used up, stars die.

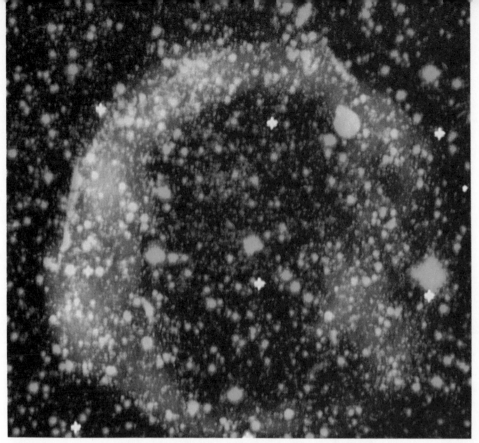

A remnant from Tycho's Supernova

When some of the biggest stars die, they blow up with a brilliant burst of light. These sensational exploding stars are called supernovas.

After exploding, one of these huge stars may shrink to a very small, super-heavy ball that has tremendous gravity. (Gravity is a force that pulls objects toward the center of a star or planet.) The ball's gravity is so powerful that it sucks in everything nearby. Not even starlight can escape this monstrous pull. Since no light can escape from this shrunken ball, it cannot be seen. It is known as a black hole.

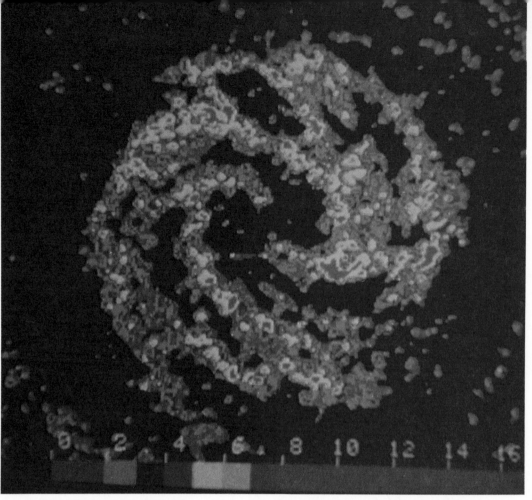

Many galaxies, including our Milky Way, look like spirals.

## GALAXIES

Our planet, Earth, is located within a huge star group called the Milky Way Galaxy. Our galaxy has more than 100 billion stars. That is 20 stars for each man, woman, and child in the world.

Our Milky Way Galaxy spins around. It also flies through space like a giant Frisbee, at a speed of more than a million miles an hour.

The Great Galaxy in Andromeda

The Milky Way Galaxy is enormous. If a starship could fly at the speed of light from one side of the galaxy to the other, it would still need more than 100,000 years to complete the trip.

The farthest place in space that we can see with our eyes alone is the Great Galaxy in Andromeda. If aliens there sent a message to Earth at light speed, we wouldn't get it for 2 million years. To see the galaxies beyond Andromeda, we must use telescopes.

## TELESCOPES

You would need the power
of a million eyes to see as far
and as clearly as giant
telescopes. A giant telescope in
New York could read the "1"
on a dollar bill being held up
in Florida.

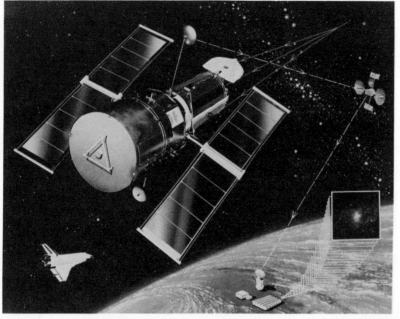

Space telescopes are
launched into space to look at
distant stars and galaxies.
These telescopes pick up more
starlight and work better than
telescopes on Earth because
Earth's air and clouds don't
block their view.

A space telescope sends information to scientists on Earth.

The Arecibo radio telescope

Radio telescopes use big bowl-shaped receivers to pick up radio signals from space. Astronomers use those signals to get a picture of distant galaxies. Radio telescopes must be big to pick up signals across trillions of miles. The world's biggest single bowl-shaped receiver is near Arecibo, Puerto Rico. Over 350 million boxes of cereal could fit inside its bowl.

Saturn

Neptune

## OUR SOLAR SYSTEM

Thousands of objects travel around the sun. The biggest are planets, including Earth. The smallest are bits of rock and dust. The sun and all the objects that circle it make up our solar system.

The nine planets in our solar system go around the sun in enormous loops, or orbits, like runners in track lanes. One trip around the sun by a planet is a year on that planet. Earth takes 365 days—one Earth year—to circle the sun.

Our sun is a star. It is only a medium-sized star, but it gives off more light than 3,800 billion trillion light bulbs shining all at once. Its light shines farther than the planet Pluto, which is 4 billion miles away.

Our sun

While the planets travel around the sun, they also spin around and around like gigantic tops. When the sun shines on one side of a planet, that side has daylight. The side away from the sun is in darkness. One whole turn is called a day on each planet. Earth takes 24 hours—one Earth day—to make a complete spin.

Mercury

## MERCURY

Mercury circles the sun the fastest of all the planets. A year on Mercury lasts just 88 Earth days. If you lived on Mercury, you would have lots of birthdays. If you were eight years old on Earth, you'd be thirty-three years old on Mercury.

Mercury has many craters that were blasted out by rocks crashing down from space long ago. The biggest crater, Caloris Basin, is 930 miles across. The states of Texas, California, and Montana could all fit inside it.

This painting shows a scientific probe near Venus.

# VENUS

Venus is the hottest planet. Thick clouds around the planet trap sunshine so the temperature is 900 degrees Fahrenheit. The air on Venus is poisonous.

A day lasts longer than a year on Venus. Venus spins around so slowly that one Venus day lasts as long as 243 Earth days. Venus goes around the sun in less time than it takes to spin around once. A year on Venus—one trip around the sun—lasts only 225 Earth days.

# EARTH

Earth is the only planet we know of that has living creatures. It is 93 million miles from the sun—an ideal location. Earth is far enough from the sun so that we don't burn up in its intense heat. And yet, Earth is close enough to the sun so that we have the warmth we need to live.

A view of Earth from space

Earth's moon is the only place in space that humans have stepped on. Astronaut Neil Armstrong walked on our moon in 1969, and his footprints are likely to still be there millions of years from now. Since there is no air, water, wind, or rain on the moon, only space dust disturbs the footprints.

Neil Armstrong's footprint on the moon

## MARS

Mars has a volcano named Olympus Mons (Mount Olympus), which is the biggest volcano ever seen in our solar system. It is 16 miles high. The top of it blew off long ago and left a crater 50 miles wide.

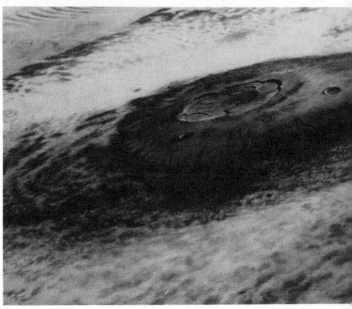

Olympus Mons on Mars

Every person in the United States could park two cars inside the crater of Olympus Mons.

Mars also has a canyon 3,000 miles long—the biggest one we know of. If it were on Earth, this canyon, Mariner Valley, would stretch across the United States from Washington, D.C., to San Francisco.

Jupiter

## JUPITER

Jupiter is the largest planet. More than 1,400 Earths could fit inside Jupiter if it were hollow.

Jupiter has a big reddish oval shape on top of its clouds that we call the Great Red Spot. This red spot is three times as big as Earth. It is actually a huge storm that has raged for more than 300 years.

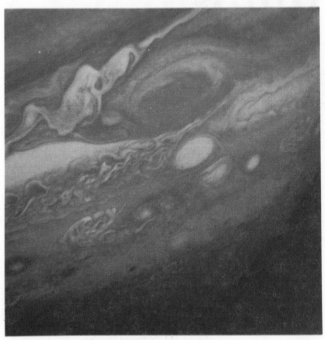

The Great Red Spot

This painting shows a *Voyager* spacecraft passing Saturn.

## SATURN

Saturn is the planet with the most objects circling it. It has ten large moons, many small moons, and dazzling rings. The rings are not solid. They are made of billions of chunks of ice and rock that shine in sunlight.

A painting of a *Voyager* spacecraft passing Uranus

## URANUS

The narrow rings around Uranus may be the remains of a moon that crashed into the planet or was torn up by Uranus' gravity. The rings are made of chunks of ice and rock, with a lot of dust in between.

Uranus looks blue, but its clouds are really made of colorless gases. The clouds get their color because one of the gases, methane, absorbs the red light contained in sunlight. When the red light is absorbed, the blue light in the sunlight shows up more.

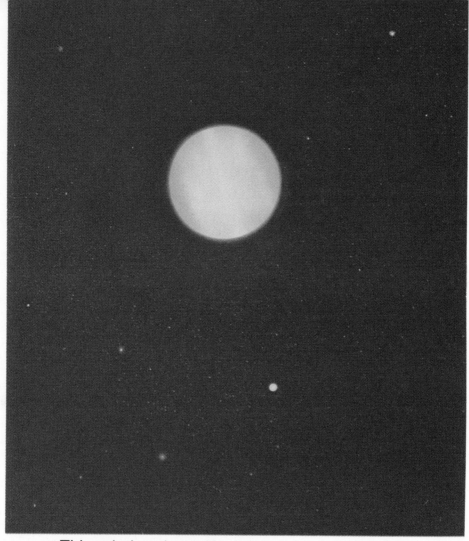

This painting shows Neptune and its moon Triton.

## NEPTUNE

Neptune is the farthest planet from the sun today. Pluto usually holds that record. But, in 1980, Pluto crossed inside Neptune's orbit, moving closer to the sun. It will cross out again in 1999.

No human could live to be one year old on Neptune. The planet takes 164 Earth years to circle the sun.

# PLUTO

Pluto is called a planet, but it is much smaller than the other planets and follows a strange orbit. Pluto may actually be a moon that escaped Neptune's gravity. Or it could be a rocky iceball that was captured by our sun's gravity as it wandered by our solar system.

Pluto's path marks the outer boundary of our solar system. It is 4 billion miles from the sun. In 1983 *Pioneer 10* became the first spacecraft to cross the boundary. *Pioneer 10* traveled eleven years to get from Earth to the boundary.

A painting of Pluto, its moon, Charon, and, in the distance, the sun

# YOUR SPACE ADDRESS

The biggest group of objects in the universe is a supercluster. It is a large group of many clusters of galaxies.

You can write your own space address by filling in the blanks below.

_____
(name)

_____
(number and street)

_____
(city and state)

_____
(country)

Planet Earth
Solar System
Milky Way Galaxy
Local Group
Virgo Supercluster